P9-CWD-859

CHICKEN SOUP for LITTLE SOULS

The Goodness Gorillas

Story Adapted from "Practice Random
Acts of Kindness and Senseless Acts
of Beauty" by Adair Lara

Story Adaptation by
Lisa McCourt

Illustrated by
Pat Grant Porter

HCI

Health Communications, Inc.
Deerfield Beach, Florida

Library of Congress Cataloging-in-Publication Data

McCourt, Lisa.
    Chicken soup for little souls : the Goodness Gorillas / story adaptation by Lisa McCourt ;
illustrations by Pat Porter.
        p.   cm.
    "Based on the . . . best-selling series Chicken soup for the soul by Jack Canfield and Mark
Victor Hansen."
    Summary: Jessica and her classmates form a club whose mission is to perform acts of
kindness, even for the meanest boy in the class.
    ISBN 1-55874-505-X (hardcover)
    [1. Kindness—Fiction. 2. Clubs—Fiction. 3. Conduct of life—Fiction. 4. Schools—Fiction.]
    I. Porter, Pat Grant, ill. II. Canfield, Jack, date. Chicken soup for the soul. III. Title.
    PZ7.M13745Ch   1997
    [E]—dc21   97-19959
                                                                          CIP
                                                                          AC

©1997 Health Communications, Inc.
ISBN 1-55874-505-X

Story adapted from "Practice Random Acts of Kindness and Senseless Acts of Beauty" by Adair Lara,
A 2nd Helping of Chicken Soup for the Soul™, edited by Jack Canfield and Mark Victor Hansen.

Story Adaptation ©1997 Lisa McCourt
Illustrations ©1997 Pat Grant Porter

Cover Design by Cheryl Nathan

Produced by Boingo Books, Inc.

Publisher: Health Communications, Inc.
             3201 S.W. 15th Street
             Deerfield Beach, FL 33442-8190

Printed in Mexico

It started the day Jessica Docket brought cupcakes to school for the whole class.

"Jessica!" said Ms. King. "I didn't know it was your birthday."

"It's not. My mom made cupcakes because she's a gorilla."

Jessica handed Ms. King a note.

Ms. King wrote these words on the chalkboard: guerrilla goodness.

Dear Ms. King
Thank you for letting me practice guerrilla goodness on your class.
Ms. Docket

She told the class, "We all know what a gorilla is. But this word, guerrilla, means something else. It's a word that people use when they are part of a group that is trying to change something."

"Like a secret club?" asked Patricia.

"Sort of like that. Guerrilla goodness means practicing random acts of kindness. That's what Ms. Docket and lots of other people all over the world are doing right now. They're trying to make the world a nicer place just by finding new ways to be extra kind and good to people— even to strangers."

"You mean Ms. Docket makes cupcakes for strangers, too?" asked Stuart.

"She might. Or she might let someone in front of her in line at the grocery store..."

"She might shovel snow from her neighbors' driveways without saying anything. She might plant flowers in a public place for everyone to enjoy, or help poor people. There are lots of ways to spread goodness once you start looking for them."

At lunch time, everyone was talking about guerrilla goodness.

"Real gorillas in the jungle do nice things for each other, too," said Tina. "I saw it on TV."

"Let's make our own club!" said Michael. "Jessica should be the leader since she knows the most about it."

And that's how the Goodness Gorillas started.

Peter came to school early and sharpened all his classmates' pencils. Everyone smiled and said, "Thanks, Peter!"

Everyone except Todd. He tried to poke Peter in the arm with his pencil's new sharp point.

Jessica pulled out a mat for every person in her gymnastics class. "What a lovely act of kindness," said her coach.

Stuart let his little sister watch her favorite TV show, even though it was his turn to choose the channel. Later that night, his sister gave him the last piece of her Halloween candy.

All of the Goodness Gorillas met on Sunday and cleaned up the litter in the park. They were having a great time until Todd showed up with his scary dog, Brutus. Todd laughed hard when Brutus nipped at Jessica's heels and growled at all the children.

Todd walked over to the pile of cans the Goodness Gorillas had gathered for recycling. He picked them up, one by one, and threw them all over the park. "Hey, dumb Gorillas, go fetch!" he yelled.

"Why does Todd always have to be so mean?" asked Tina.

The Goodness Gorillas picked up all the cans again, but it wasn't as much fun as it had been before.

Patricia cleaned her room and her brother's room without being asked. Her dad thanked her and made her favorite dinner.

Tina packed up all her old toys and her mom helped her bring them to a homeless shelter. "I'm so proud of you," said her mom.

Michael went with his uncle to volunteer at a senior citizen's home. A lady there told him, "You made our day."

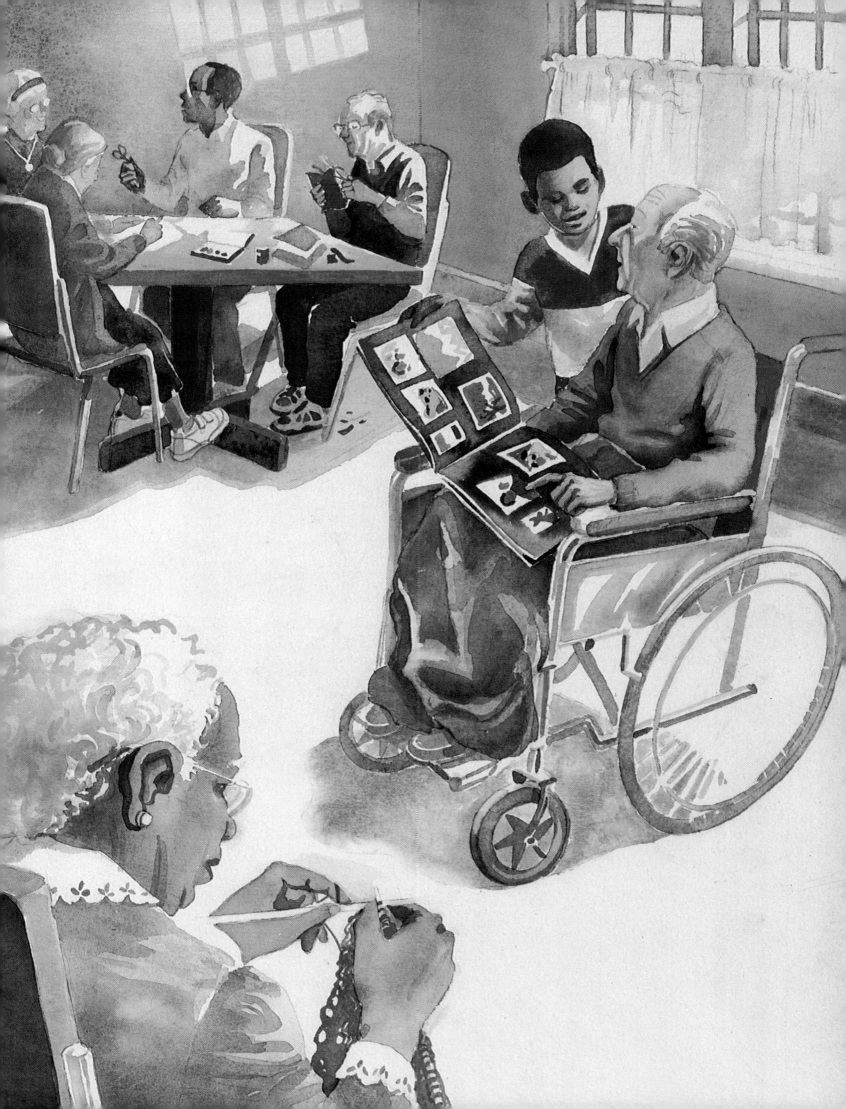

The Goodness Gorillas met at recess every day to talk about new ideas for spreading kindness. And every day Todd danced around the group, grunting and scratching his armpits.

"Oo—oo—oo—oo! Look at me—I'm a gorilla! I'm a big, dumb gorilla who makes goody-good with everyone!"

"What a creep," said Stuart. "All he ever does is cause trouble."

"Go away, Todd!" said Jessica. "If you can't be nice, we don't want you around."

One day, Ms. King said, "I have some sad news, class. Yesterday afternoon, Todd's dog, Brutus, was hit by a car. He died in the night. Todd is at home feeling bad and very alone. I'm hoping some of you will visit him. Does that sound like a job for the Goodness Gorillas?"

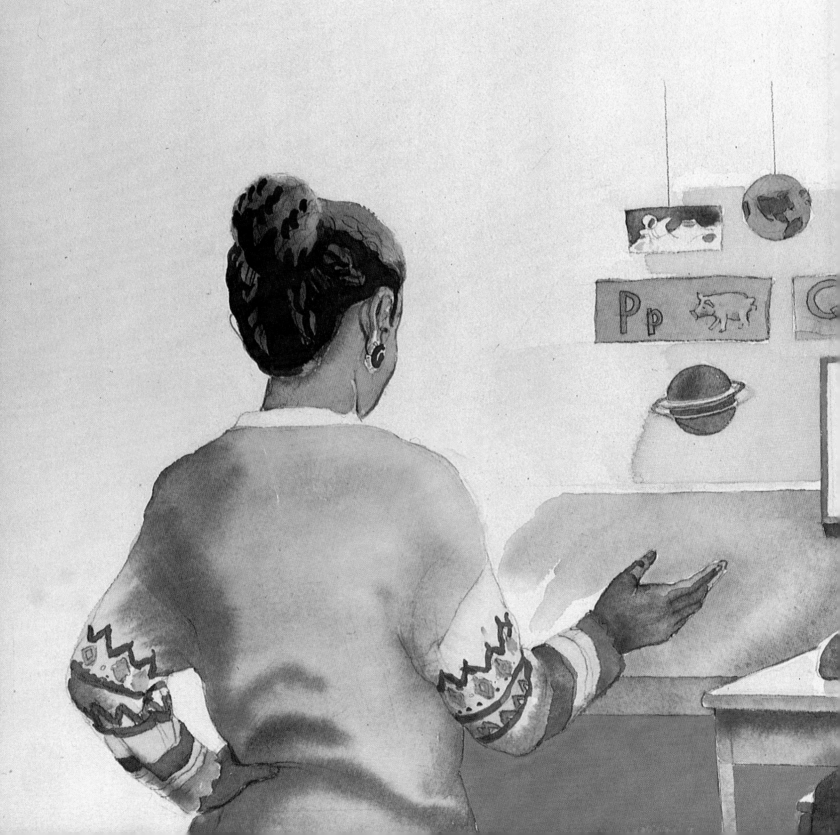

Jessica raised her hand. "It's just that...Todd makes fun of us so much. I wouldn't know what to say if we visited him."

"Maybe he's felt left out," said Ms. King. "Did any of you ever ask Todd if he'd like to join your club?"

"He's not a Goodness Gorilla!" cried Tina. "He's a Meanness Monster!"

"Goodness Gorillas see the good in everyone," said Ms. King. "Isn't that what you told me, Jessica?"

At recess, the Goodness Gorillas tried to decide what to do. Even though he'd been rotten, they all felt really bad for Todd. Brutus was his only friend.

"I know!" said Jessica. "My mom could take us to the pound to find a new dog for Todd!"

"Except," said Peter, "spreading kindness means spreading it to animals, too. I'd feel sorry for any dog we gave to Todd!"

"We'll just have to find some good in Todd first then," said Jessica. "I have a plan. Tonight every one of us will write down one good thing about Todd. I know it's hard, but try! And remember: there's good in everybody."

The next day, all the Goodness Gorillas stood on Todd's doorstep and rang the doorbell. Todd answered the door himself. He looked like he'd been crying. "What do you want?" he asked.

"We've come to make you a Goodness Gorilla!" said Jessica.

Todd narrowed his eyes. "Why?" he growled, looking nastier than ever.

"Let us in and we'll tell you all the reasons."

Todd turned around and stomped back into the house, but he left the door open. The Goodness Gorillas piled in, each one carrying a piece of paper.

"Todd's the fastest runner in our class," said Patricia.

"Todd has nice blue eyes," said Tina.

"Todd was friendly back in first grade," said Stuart.

"Todd is funny when he tells jokes that don't make fun of people," said Peter.

"Michael and I came up with the same reason," said Jessica. "And it's the best one of all: Todd does a great gorilla imitation!"

"We want to learn it!" said Michael and Tina and Peter. "We all want to be gorillas!"

"How do you make the grunts sound so real? Show us how to do the hop!" said Patricia.

Everyone tried to do Todd's gorilla dance while Todd
stood and watched them. Finally he had to smile, and then
laugh. They weren't making fun of him. They really
wanted to learn!

When he couldn't resist any longer, Todd turned himself into a gorilla too. Everyone followed his lead. They all grunted and hopped and scratched and screeched until they fell, out of breath and laughing, into a big heap on the floor.

Jessica said, "Now that you're one of us, Todd, we have a surprise for you!" She took Todd's arm and led him out to his back yard, where the Goodness Gorillas had tied a furry, funny, black-and-white puppy.

Todd ran over to the puppy and knelt down beside her, hugging her and stroking her fur. Big tears filled his eyes when he looked up at his new friends. "I'm sorry I made fun of you," he said. "I didn't think you would ever be this nice to *me*. Can I really join your club?"

The puppy jumped up and down.

"Look! She wants to be a gorilla, too!" said Tina.

"That's what I'll name her!" said Todd. "Her name can be G.G.—for Goodness Gorillas—and she can belong to the whole club, like a mascot!"

Everyone loved the idea.

The Goodness Gorillas signed up more and more members. Ms. King's class became a nicer place. Then the school became a nicer place, and then the town did.

And as the Goodness Gorillas grew up, and went to different colleges, and traveled to different cities...the whole world became a nicer place.